TITANIC
The Story of a Disaster

Dee Phillips

SADDLEBACK
PUBLISHING

Yesterday's Voices

Gladiator
Holocaust
Over the Top
Runaway
Tail Gunner
Titanic

© Copyright Ruby Tuesday Books Limited 2013
This edition is published by arrangement with ReadZone Books Limited.

Images are in the public domain, or courtesy of Shutterstock and Superstock (pages 41, 43).

Acknowledgements: With thanks to Lorraine Petersen, Chief Executive of NASEN, for her help in the development and creation of these books.

www.sdlback.com

ISBN-13: 978-1-62250-877-8
ISBN-10: 1-62250-877-7
eBook: 978-1-63078-012-8

Printed in Guangzhou, China
NOR/1213/CA21302310

18 17 16 15 14   1 2 3 4 5

The ship is slowly sinking.
I don't want to die in the icy black water.
When will help come?

TITANIC
The Story of a Disaster

In April 1912 the largest ship the world had ever seen set sail on her first voyage.

She was sailing from England to America.

Some passengers were taking a luxury vacation.

Others were traveling to a new life in America.

The ship was named

TITANIC...

...and she would never reach America.

I am so cold.
So cold and scared.
I hear men shouting.
Women are crying.

I look over the railing
into the black water.
The ship is slowly sinking.

I don't want to die.
I don't want to die
in the icy black water.

I am so cold.
So cold and scared.
The ship is slowly sinking.
When will help come?

I need to find my brother.

Where are you, Edward?
Please come and take care of me.

Mother died when I was a child.
So Edward took care of me.

When Father beat me, Edward
wiped away my tears.

I was never scared if
Edward was there.

I am so cold.
So cold and scared.

I look over the railing
into the icy black water.
I wait on the deck of the ship.

Where are you, Edward?
Please come and take care of me.

When I was 16, I fell in love.
He was a gardener at the
big house.

I knew what we did was wrong.
But then it was too late.

I was so scared.
I knew Father would beat
me when he found out.

Edward wiped away my tears.
He said, "I will take care of you, Maggie."

I worked as a maid at the big house.
The mistress was young and kind.

She said, "We are going to visit
America, Maggie."

"We are going on a new ship.
I want you to come with us."

I didn't know what to do.
My dress was growing tighter.
Father would beat me.

Edward said, "I will come
with you to America.
I'll get work on the ship.
I will take care of you, Maggie.
You and your baby."

Titanic was the most beautiful place
I'd ever seen.

My cabin was bigger than our whole cottage.
I helped the mistress unpack her silk dresses.

My own dress was growing tighter.
But soon we would be in America.
Edward would take care of me
and my baby.

I went to Southampton with Maggie.
Titanic was the biggest ship I'd ever seen.
I waited on the dock.
Some lads had not shown up to work.

A man asked me, "Are you a stoker?"
I didn't know what a stoker did,
but I said yes!

The ship's boiler room was hot and dark.
It was in the deepest part of the ship.
It was the most hellish place I'd ever seen.

Hour after hour, I worked.
Shoveling coal to keep the boilers burning.

But soon we would be in America.
I would take care of Maggie.
Maggie and her baby.

It was my fifth night on the ship.
Suddenly I woke up.
I didn't know why.
The engines had stopped.
The mistress came into my cabin.

"Something bad has happened," she said.
"I want you to come with me.
We must go up on deck."

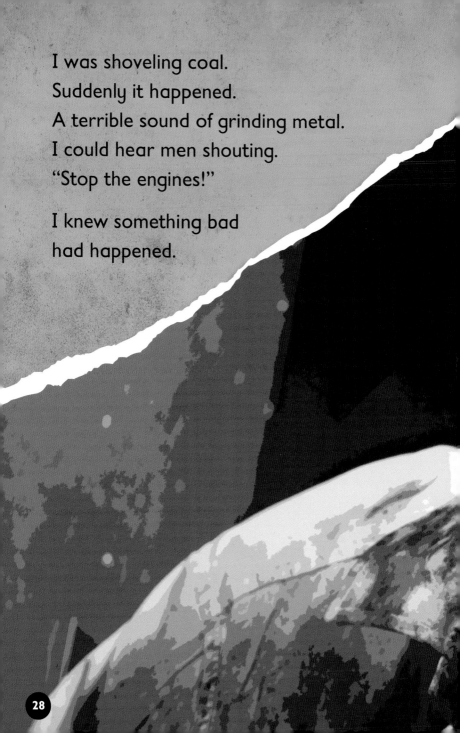

I was shoveling coal.
Suddenly it happened.
A terrible sound of grinding metal.
I could hear men shouting.
"Stop the engines!"

I knew something bad
had happened.

I am so cold.
So cold and scared.
I wait on the deck of the ship.
The mistress climbed into a lifeboat.

She said, "I want you to come with me, Maggie."

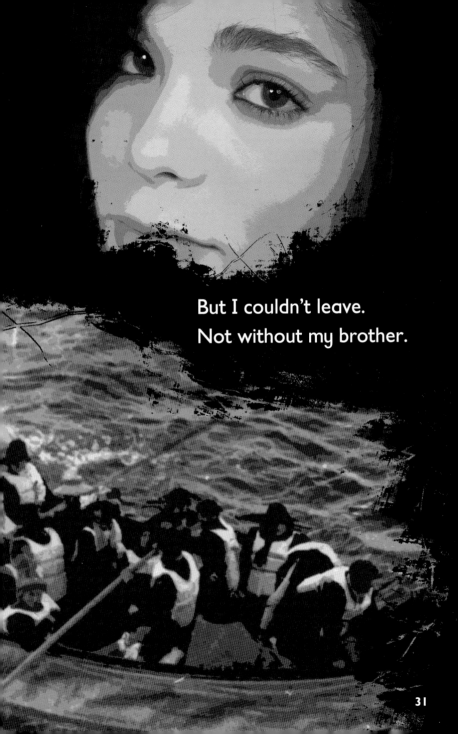

But I couldn't leave.
Not without my brother.

I am so scared.
All around me there is steam and smoke.
The lads are shouting.
They say the ship is sinking.
But we have to keep the boilers burning.

The boilers keep the pumps working.
Without the pumps, the ship will
sink even faster.

But I want to find my sister.
Where are you, Maggie?

They say we hit an iceberg.
The ship is sinking into the
icy black water.

Some people escape in lifeboats.
But there are not enough
for everyone.
People scream as they fall
from the deck.

I hold on tight to a railing.
Edward will find me soon.
He has to.
Help will come soon.
It has to.

They say *Titanic* hit an iceberg.
The iceberg tore a huge hole in her side.
We kept the boilers burning.
We kept the pumps working.
But it was not enough.
The ship is sinking.

The boiler room is filling with water.
There's no chance for us lads down here.

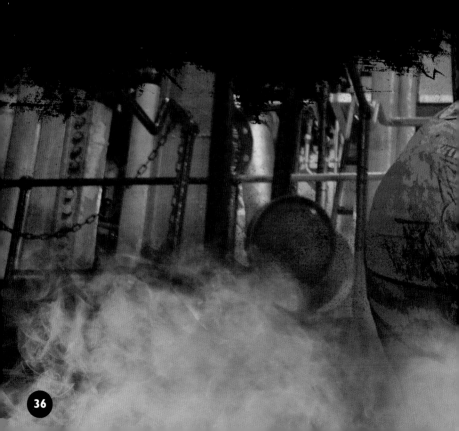

The icy black water fills my nose and mouth.
I can't breathe.
But I know you will be safe, Maggie.
You will be safe in a lifeboat.

Make a good life in America, Maggie.
I'm sorry, Maggie.

I am so cold.
So cold and scared.

I'm sinking into the icy black water.
I don't want to die.
I don't want my baby to die.

Someone please help me.
Someone please help us all.

TITANIC

Behind the Story

The *RMS Titanic* left Southampton on April 10, 1912, bound for America. On board were more than 2,200 passengers and crew.

At 11:40 p.m. on April 14, *Titanic* struck an iceberg in the Atlantic Ocean. The iceberg tore a nearly 250-foot gash in the ship. The crew soon realized that their new ship, which the world believed was unsinkable, was taking on water and sinking fast.

The ship's lifeboats were launched, with women and children given priority. There were not enough lifeboats, however, to hold everyone. Also, many lifeboats rowed away from the sinking ship half empty. The people left behind knew they were doomed. The men working in the boiler and engine rooms deep below deck stayed at their posts. They knew they would have no chance to escape when the end came.

Titanic sank in just two hours 40 minutes. There was no time for other ships to come to her rescue. Just over 700 people in the lifeboats survived and were later rescued by a ship called the *Carpathia*. More than 1,500 people drowned in the icy Atlantic Ocean.

Titanic's passengers traveled in first, second, or third class. Many first class passengers were wealthy Americans who had been touring Europe. Many of the third class, or steerage, passengers were extremely poor people from Ireland. Some had sold everything they owned to buy a ticket to a new life in America.

TITANIC
What's next?

FLASHBACK
ON YOUR OWN

Maggie and Edward tell their stories using flashbacks. Movies often use flashbacks as a way to explain how a character came to be in a place or situation. Write a story that uses flashbacks. Think about:

- Where is your main character in the present day?

- What is the character feeling?

- Use flashbacks to explain the character's situation and how he or she is feeling.

TWO SIDES TO EVERY STORY
WITH A PARTNER

Maggie and Edward both talk about the same event but from different viewpoints. With a partner, choose an event to talk about. It could be a concert you both went to or something that happened in your town. Each write down five memories of the event. Then take turns reading a sentence out loud.

- How are your memories alike? How are they different?

Maggie and Edward are characters in a story. Their story, however, is based on what happened to hundreds of people the night the *Titanic* sank. Discuss with your group how the story makes you feel. Think about:

- What did it feel like to be trapped on the ship knowing you would drown?

- The *Titanic* disaster happened more than 100 years ago. Why do you think people today are still so interested in the story?

DISCOVERING TITANIC
ON YOUR OWN / WITH A PARTNER

In 1985 underwater archaeologist Dr. Robert Ballard discovered the wreck of the *Titanic*.

Go online to find out more about Dr. Ballard's expeditions and to see photos and videos of the wreck of the *Titanic*.

This photo shows the bow, or front, of the *Titanic*.

Titles in the

Yesterday's Voices

series

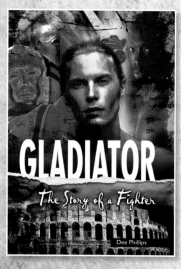

I waited deep below the arena.
Then it was my turn to fight.
Kill or be killed!

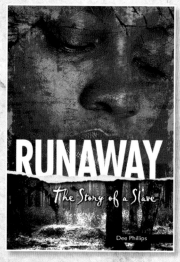

I cannot live as a slave
any longer. Tonight I will
escape and never go back.

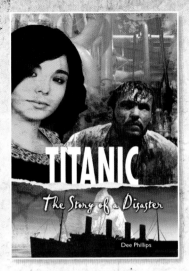

TITANIC
The Story of a Disaster
Dee Phillips

The ship is sinking into the icy sea. I don't want to die. Someone help us!

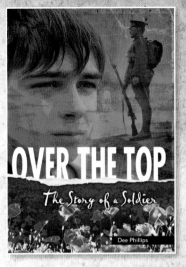

OVER THE TOP
The Story of a Soldier
Dee Phillips

I'm waiting in the trench. I am so afraid. Tomorrow we go over the top.

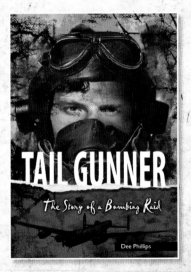

TAIL GUNNER
The Story of a Bombing Raid
Dee Phillips

Another night. Another bombing raid. Will this night be the one when we don't make it back?

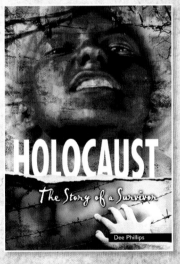

HOLOCAUST
The Story of a Survivor
Dee Phillips

They took my clothes and shaved my head. I was no longer a human.